For Rory, Peter and Brian

Also by Oliver Jeffers

First published in hardback in Great Britain by HarperCollins Children's Books in 2005
First published in paperback in 2006

20

ISBN-13: 978-0-00-715036-6

HarperCollins Children's Books is a division of HarperCollins Publishers Ltd.
The author/illustrator asserts the moral right to be identified as the author/illustrator
of the work. A CIP catalogue record for this title is available from the British Library.

Visit our website at: www.harpercollins.co.uk

Printed in Italy

Lost and Found

Oliver Jeffers

HarperCollins *Children's Books*

Once there was a boy

and one day he found a penguin at his door.

The boy didn't know where it had come from

but it began to follow him everywhere.

The penguin looked sad and
the boy thought it must be lost.

So the boy decided to help the penguin
find its way home.

He checked in the Lost and Found Office.
But no one was missing a penguin.

He asked some birds if they knew
where the penguin came from.

But they ignored him.
Some birds are like that.

The boy asked his duck.

But the duck floated away.
He didn't know.

That night, the boy couldn't sleep for disappointment. He wanted to help the penguin but he didn't know how.

The next morning he discovered that
penguins come from the South Pole.
But how could he get there?

He ran down to the harbour and asked a
big ship to take them to the South Pole.
But his voice was much too small to
be heard over the ship's horn.

So together, he and the penguin would row to the South Pole. The boy took his rowboat out of the cupboard and they tested it for size and strength.

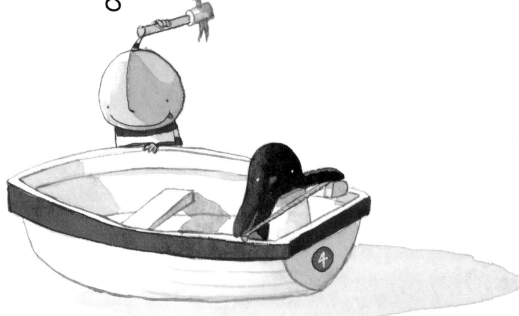

They packed everything they would need...

and together they pushed
the rowboat out to sea.

They rowed south for many days...

and nights with the boy telling stories all the way. The penguin listened to everything that the boy said.

They floated through good weather and bad,

when the waves were as big as mountains...

...until they came to the South Pole.

The boy was delighted,
but the penguin said nothing.
Suddenly it looked sad again as
the boy helped it out of the boat.

The boy said goodbye...

and floated away. But as he looked back,
the penguin looked sadder than ever.

It felt strange to be on his own...

and the more he thought...

...the more he realised he was making a big mistake.

The penguin wasn't lost. He was just lonely.

Quickly he turned the boat around
and headed back to the South Pole
as fast as he could.

At last he reached
the Pole again.
But where was
the penguin?

The boy searched
and searched but
he was nowhere
to be found.

Sadly the boy set off for home.

There was no point telling stories
because there was no one to listen,
except the wind and the waves.

But then the boy saw something
in the water ahead of him.
Closer and closer he got,
until he could see...

...the penguin.

And so the boy and his friend went
home together, talking of wonderful
things all the way.